AUTUMN
PUBLISHING

Published in 2022
First published in the UK by Autumn Publishing
An imprint of Igloo Books Ltd
Cottage Farm, NN6 0BJ, UK
Owned by Bonnier Books
Sveavägen 56, Stockholm, Sweden
www.autumnpublishing.co.uk

0122 001
2 4 6 8 10 9 7 5 3 1
ISBN 978-1-80022-271-7

Written by Marnie Willow
Illustrated by Jana Curll

Edited by Helen Catt
Designed by Chris Stanley
Inclusion consultancy by Cathy Atkinson

Printed and manufactured in China

ANYONE CAN BE MY FRIEND

AUTUMN
PUBLISHING

On this giant spinning ball,

From Montreal to Senegal,

Live eight billion people, all in all.

8,000,

Some are old and some are small,

Some are short and some are tall,

Some can run and some just crawl . . .

0,00,000

. . . But most amazingly of all . . .

. . . Anyone could be my friend.

The world's a big place for a bear,
And my friend could be anywhere.
I'll sail by ship or fly by air,
And hope my friend is waiting there.

Someone to love, someone who'll care,
There's countless people out, out there,
But a bear just needs one special friend.

They could live in any place,
In any country, any state,
Perhaps they live near trees and lakes,
Or by a busy marketplace . . .

"Can I fit this in my suitcase?"

I might not know their name or face, but somewhere, somehow I'll find my friend.

I don't know what they'll like to wear,

Or how they'll like to style their hair.

Perhaps, they'll decorate their chair
With ribbons and fantastic flair,
As long as there is room to spare,
Inside their heart for one small bear,
We'll make a super stylish pair . . .

. . . Me (the bear) and my new friend.

Perhaps there is a family
That has a bit more room for me:
A dad or mum, or two, or three.

As long as "I" can be a "we"
And we can sit beside the sea,
Or underneath a shady tree,
There'll be no better family,
To love and care for my new friend.

I wonder what they'll like to eat,

If they like vegetables or meat,

Mild and cool or spicy heat,

Or if they'd like a something-sweet,

As an extra-special treat,

From the stall that's down their street.

Either way, I can't wait to meet,
And share a treat with my new friend.

They'll celebrate in different ways,
A hundred different special days,
With twinkling lights . . .

. . . Or bright bouquets . . .

. . . With coloured paints in
rainbow shades . . .

. . . or Christmas trees and jingling sleighs.

I'll always find myself amazed,
that on each and all these special days . . .

However far I have to roam,
I'll find a person of my own,
Who'll pick me up and take me home.

No more wandering all alone,
Across the great and grand unknown,
Although I think I may have shown,
I wasn't really *that* alone.

The ships are sailed,
the flights are flown.

I'm safe and
home . . .

. . . with my
new friend.

Talking to your child about inclusivity and diversity

Inclusivity and diversity are big, complex ideas, and the process of teaching your child about them may feel daunting. Fortunately, from a very early age, children are naturally open to new experiences and meeting new people.

As they grow, your child will encounter people whose race or ethnicity, gender, sexuality or ability is different from theirs. While your child is very young, one of the best things you can do is give them plenty of opportunities to meet people of different backgrounds.

Encourage respectful curiosity. If your child asks you a question you don't know the answer to, you can find out together. You can enjoy learning about other cultures' holidays and festivals throughout the year, and if invited, you may wish to join or attend. Food is another channel through which people are often open to sharing their culture, and is often appealing to children.

Be mindful of the books, TV shows, films and other media that you show to your child. Try to choose examples that mirror the world at its best and most inclusive. Expose them to a variety of positive role models, in real life and in media, sports or culture. Show them that anyone can be anything or do anything that they dream of.

Inclusivity isn't something you can teach your child overnight. Remember always to encourage your child to be kind and curious about this incredible, remarkable world and all eight billion of its residents.